The
WITCHES
of
BENEVENTO

The WITCHES of BENEVENTO

THE SECRET JANARA

A Primo Story

VIKING

VIKING

An imprint of Penguin Random House LLC, New York

First published in the United States of America by Viking,
an imprint of Penguin Random House LLC, 2019

Visit us online at penguinrandomhouse.com

LIBRARY OF CONGRESS CATALOGING-IN-PUBLICATION DATA
Names: Marciano, John Bemelmans, author. | Blackall, Sophie, illustrator. Title:
The secret Janara / written by John Bemelmans Marciano ; illustrated by Sophie Blackall.
Description: New York : Viking published by Penguin Group, [2019] | Series: The witches
of Benevento ; 6 | Summary: Primo finds a clue to the identity of the secret Janara, a bottle
of the oil that a Janara needs to transform, but what will he do with the knowledge? |
Identifiers: LCCN 2018036115 (print) | LCCN 2018041980 (ebook) |
ISBN 9780425291559 (ebook) | ISBN 9780425291542 (hardback)
Subjects: | CYAC: Witches—Fiction. | Magic—Fiction. | Fantasy. | BISAC:
JUVENILE FICTION / Fantasy & Magic. | JUVENILE FICTION / Imagination &
Play. | JUVENILE FICTION / Action & Adventure / General. Classification: LCC PZ7.
M328556 (ebook) | LCC PZ7.M328556 Sec 2019 (print) | DDC [Fic]—dc23
LC record available at https://lccn.loc.gov/2018036115

1 3 5 7 9 10 8 6 4 2

Manufactured in China   Set in IM FELL French Canon
Book design by Nancy Brennan

To Paola Caruso

—J.B.M. and S.B.

Emilio

Rosa

Primo

Maria Beppina

Sergio

CONTENTS

THESE BOOKS ARE LIKE PUZZLES!

LOOK FOR THE FRAMES IN EACH BOOK...

...AND JOIN UP THE PICTURES!

There's this boy—you know the kind—who always has to be the center of attention. He's the sort who thinks the entire world revolves around him. Or that it <u>should</u>.

He wants to be great. He wants to be a HERO.

But can he even be the hero of his own tale?

This boy dreams and he schemes, and schemes and he dreams.

But what happens when he realizes that none of his dreams will ever come true?

And then what happens when—even worse—one of them DOES?

Let's have a look, shall we?

YOUR
EVER-VIGILANT VIRGIL,
SIGISMUNDO

BENEV

THE TRIG

THE WELL

CEMETERY

ZIA PIA'S

THE THEATER

WHERE EVERYONE
DOES THEIR LAUNDRY

GOOD MUSHROOM PICKING

THE SECRET JANARA

A Primo Story

Before we begin . . .

THE Twins' mom is having the baby.

And it's going to ruin the whole plan!

The plan being raiding the garden of the Crones and picking it clean. For revenge!

Those rotten Crones are always ordering things from the stand and not paying. And why?

"The tomatoes were bruised!" they say, or, "The eggs were cracked!" And they always blame it on Primo, saying he's too reckless with the deliveries. Which is almost never true!

But now the Twins are running off, and— *uh-oh*—one of the shutters in the Crones' house slams open! It's the tall skinny one—the one who always stiffs them.

They're gonna get caught! Or Sergio is, anyway. He's stuck inside the garden. Primo hops down off the tree to the top of the wall and runs to get Maria Beppina.

At least he can save *her*.

1

STRONGA

RIGHT now, Primo's father is reciting.

"It was ten thousand years ago. The great Diomedes traveled far and wide until he came to the place where the rivers Sabato and Calore join. The hero stopped and said, *This is the most beautiful land I have ever seen, and I have traveled the world lo these many years since leaving Troy. I shall found a city here, and I shall name it BENEVENTO!* And then he took out the Golden Tusk of the Calydonian Boar that he had killed and planted it on this very spot!"

Maria Beppina and Isidora clap, and Primo too.

Not Uncle Tommaso, though.

"No no **no**, that's all wrong!"he says, exasperated by Poppa's ad-libbing. "First off, the tusk wasn't made of gold—the *trophy* is made of gold. Fake gold! And Diomedes didn't kill the boar! Atalanta and Meleager did."

"How do *you* know?" Primo's poppa says. "It's not like you were there!"

The eyes of Maria Beppina's father look about ready to explode out of his head.

"I don't need to have been there! It's history! *History!*"

"Ah, you can have your history! No one cares!" Poppa says. "It's all about the story. **Drama**—that's what the people want!"

What Poppa and Uncle Tommaso are arguing over is the Great Pageant of Diomedes and the Founding of Benevento, the play that gets presented right before the Boar Hunt.

The Feast of the Boar is the main festival of the Triggio. The boar is the symbol of Benevento, because of how Diomedes brought the tusk of the Calydonian Boar here. The Calydonian Boar was this terrible monster that terrorized Greece, and all the ancient heroes like Jason and Theseus got together and hunted it, which is the inspiration for the Boar Hunt—the most awesome thing that ever happens in the Triggio.

At least, this is what Primo thinks. For Poppa, the most awesome thing is this pageant. He never wanted to win the Golden Tusk when he was a boy like all the other fathers—he wanted to act in the play. He started helping when he was Primo's age, and now he is the star, stage builder, and director of the show. Uncle Tommaso is the other main actor and the scene painter. Primo helps with the building, while Isidora and Maria Beppina make the costumes.

"And it only happened two thousand seven hundred years ago, not ten thousand!" Uncle Tommaso says.

Poppa rolls his eyes. "*Two thousand seven hundred?* That's such a complicated, *boring* number! Who even knows what it means? Now ten thousand—**that** is dramatic!"

The most dramatic thing, however, is just about to happen.

"So **here** is where you all are!"

It's Momma. She's in a fury—even by Momma standards.

"I just walked by the stand and it's not open!" she says, walking up onto the stage so she can yell directly at Poppa. "How will we make money? How will we *eat*!"

"But it's the pageant!" Poppa says, as if that were explanation enough.

HOW WILL WE *EAT?*

But it's not. Not for Momma, anyway.

She tells Primo to come open the stand with her.

"Hey, no fair!" Primo says. "Why does Isidora get to stay and *I* have to work?"

But as usual, no one pays any attention to what Primo wants. As Momma drags him away, Isidora gives him a wave and a wicked grin.

Big sisters are the worst.

When they get to the stand, Emilio is there waiting.

"Hey, where were you this morning?" Emilio says to Primo. "Dino and I came to drop off the deliveries, but no one was here."

Emilio and Dino—not Rosa. Ever since the baby was born, Rosa has to stay home and help her momma take care of it, so now Dino comes with the cart. Primo will never admit it, but it's less fun not having Rosa come around.

Primo tells them how his mom dragged him away from helping with the pageant, but that he doesn't really care.

"I mean, who cares about a dumb play when this year we get to be in the Boar Hunt!"

They are *finally* old enough to enter the contest—this is the moment Primo has been waiting for his whole life! Whoever manages to capture the boar in the arena wins the Golden Tusk—the trophy—and becomes famous forever! People still talk about how the Twins' dad won it. And Primo's own uncle Beppe!

"Tomorrow is the sign-up!" Primo says to Emilio. "It's fan-*tas*-tic!"

"Yeah, fantastic," Emilio mumbles, and says he has to go.

As Primo and Momma open the stand—setting up the table, laying out the produce—he daydreams about how he is going to win the contest. He has a plan, too.

He'll volunteer to go first. That way, no one else will get the chance to catch the boar before *he* does! That's smart.

Primo also has heard that Janara and spirits can influence who wins, so he's been working on a special spell for his magic ring. First he kisses it, and then he says:

Pretty great, right?

Suddenly, Primo has the feeling that someone is standing right behind him.

"I need to talk to you . . ." a voice croaks.

Primo turns, and it's the Crone—the one who discovered them! She looms over him menacingly.

She is about to say something, when:

"You!" Momma comes over and shakes a finger in the Crone's face. "You are a thief, as far as I'm concerned! Taking things and not paying for them and blaming my poor son!"

"But I—" the Crone says.

"I am sick and tired of you and your sisters and everyone else in this town taking advantage of our family's good nature!"

"But I—" the Crone says.

"Enough of your *buts*!" Momma says. "Don't you understand? Your business is no longer welcome here! Now leave!"

The Crone, looking cowed, gathers up her

shawl under her chin and walks back down the hill.

Primo is relieved. Manalonga and Crones are scary, but mothers—they're the most terrifying beings of all!

2
THE CONTEST

"HOLD still!" Isidora says. "Can't you quit fidgeting for one instant while I finish sewing?"

No, he can't. How can Primo possibly stay still when today is the day? The day of all days! The day he finally gets to compete in the great Hunt of the Boar! The day he—

"OW!" Primo yelps. Isidora stuck him with the needle. "Hey! You did that on purpose!"

"Oh no, it was an accident," Isidora says with wide innocent eyes. Then she looks at Maria Beppina and they both burst into laughter.

"Yeah, yeah, very funny!" Primo says. "But you can't ruin my mood today. Or how awesome I look in my costume!"

All the boys in the Boar Hunt have to dress like the ancient heroes. Isidora made Primo's outfit for him, which was pretty nice of her. Not that Primo could ever bring himself to thank her.

"How awesome you look in *my* costume, you mean," Isidora says. "But wait till you see the one I made for Rosa. It puts yours to shame!"

Rosa! Primo is furious at her. She entered the Boar Hunt! How dare she? Everybody knows the contest is only for boys!

It doesn't matter though. Primo is going to beat her. He's going to beat everyone!

"Girls!" Poppa says, bursting into the house with Uncle Tommaso. He looks frantic; Uncle looks exhausted.

"Here you are! I've been searching for you everywhere! Don't you know we've been up all night working on the pageant?" Poppa says. "We need to get our costumes on. Let's go!"

As the rest leave, Nonna Jovanna comes over to Primo.

HEY, SERGIO! YOU COMING?

"Look how handsome you are!" she says, pinching his cheek. "Just like my Beppe! I had a dream last night that you won that Golden Tusk, just like he did!"

Primo fixes his laurel crown and goes outside. "Hey, Sergio!" he hollers across the street. "You coming?"

ARE YOU READY TO LOSE?

He still can't believe it, but Sergio entered the contest, too. Rosa he can understand, but *Sergio*? Of course, Sergio has been acting all strange lately, like he's someone else. Someone brave. He's become a lot more fun, but also kind of annoying.

"Are you ready to **lose**?" Sergio says, walking out of his house. He makes a muscle, showing off. Not that there's much to show. "I'm gonna lift up that Golden Tusk with one hand!"

Make that *super* annoying.

They head over to the steps of the church of the Theater where all the contestants are gathering. The blacksmith's kid is already there, and so is Mozzo. Then Rosa shows up.

"Are you ready to *lose*?" Rosa says.

"Yeah, yeah," Primo says. "Sergio already used that line."

"Really?" Rosa says. And shrugs.

They take their places for the procession, but it takes forever to get moving. But then when it starts to happen, it's really happening! Primo can hardly believe it.

The drums! The horns! The parade begins! They start to march. People lining the street cheer the contestants on, and it's like all the cheering is for **him**! Primo!

The procession ends in the central arena of the Theater. Primo is ready for the hunt, but first there's the whole pageant thing. It's so *boring*! And after that comes a long speech that is even *more* boring, and *then* Sergio's stepdad explains the rules of the hunt. Like everybody doesn't know them already!

Each contestant gets a turn to try to capture the boar. One turn lasts as long as it takes for the water to drip out of a hanging jug. When the time jug is empty, the horn blows and the next contestant goes. If no one captures the boar in the first round, the turns start over again.

Before the Town Crier can even ask for the first volunteer, Primo has his hand up. "Me! Me! **Me!**" he yells.

And he gets picked!

His heart is beating so fast it's like it's going to pop out of his chest.

He kisses his magic ring and says his spell. *O ring of the Manalonga! May your power make me stronga!*

All the other boys—and Rosa—move back into the crowd, behind the barrels that rim the arena to protect the crowd.

Suddenly, Primo feels very alone.

Except he's *not* alone.

The boar is staring at him from across the Theater, its tusks rattling the bars of its cage.

The horn blares!

The gate opens!

The boar is OUT!

Primo holds the coiled rope in his left hand and the loop in his right. He charges up to the boar, but now the boar is charging up to HIM. He tosses the loop at the beast. And misses!

Primo stops, skidding in the dry dirt and kicking up dust, and starts running the other way. Now the boar is almost on him and he whips at the animal with his rope!

The boar grunts and sits down.

Everyone in the Theater laughs.

Why are they laughing?

Then Primo realizes:

The boar is going *cacca*!

This is Primo's big chance!

Moving forward, he holds out the looped end of the rope, ready to collar the boar. He's close—*so close*! And just when he's ready to slip it around the animal's neck . . .

The boar stands up and charges right at him! Primo runs the other way, just ahead of the boar's tusks! Now he's getting chased

around in circles, and everyone in the Theater is laughing again.

He leaps up onto the stage, ripping his costume in the process, but at least he's out of the way of the boar and he can plan what to do next and—

BLAAANH!

It's the horn.

His turn is over.

Over!

How can it have all happened so quickly?

And why is everyone still laughing?

Primo is humiliated!

"Nice try, son," Poppa says, patting him on the back. He's still on the stage, in his Diomedes costume.

Having to watch everyone else go is torture.

The only good thing is that none of them—not Biaso, not Ceruzzo, not even little Efi—do any better than he did. Sergio is up next, and Primo is worried that he—being suddenly brave and all—is somehow going to win. But he does not.

He goes charging right up to the boar and—**POW!**—gets rammed and tossed up in the air by one of the boar's tusks.

OUCH!

"He'll be okay," Poppa says as Sergio gets carried out of the arena. When the hunt starts back up, all the contestants are running scared from the boar. None of *them* wants to get gored!

Primo starts to feel better. He's got a chance! It doesn't look like anyone will catch the boar in the first round.

Now Mozzo goes. His older brother won the contest last year and it's like he told him some kind of secret, because almost immediately Mozzo has the boar pinned. In fact, it looks like he's going to win—but then the boar takes off, dragging him behind until Mozzo faceplants into the pile of boar dung. *Hah!* The whole crowd roars with laughter. This is great!

Only Rosa is left to go. If she can't catch the boar, it will be Primo's turn again! And now that the boar is all tired out, he'll *definitely* be able to catch it. And no one will be laughing then. They'll be cheering!

And—and—they *are* cheering. For Rosa? She caught the boar!

She won.

Primo feels his heart sink.

The loudest cheering of all is coming from Poppa, standing right next to Primo. He's whooping and whistling.

"Why are you cheering like that for *her*?"

"Because I bet half the town a scudo she'd win!" Poppa says. "We're rich!"

"You bet **against** me?" Primo says.

"Son, I love you with all my heart," Poppa says, still clapping. "But let's be serious—you're not half as strong *or* as fast as Rosa!"

3

THE HEAD OF DIANA

IT'S late and Primo is home, sitting in the dark, staring at the head of Diana. Not that he can see her. Although the moon is full, only its glow seeps through the clouds covering the night sky.

His costume is dirty and torn, and Primo himself is filthy and scraped up. The only wound he feels, however, is from losing.

Off in the distance, he can hear the noise of the feast. Primo couldn't take being at the party, what with everyone celebrating Rosa. How many times could they toast a person? And how many times could she tell the same stupid story about tying up the boar? Didn't they realize it was only because the boar was tired that she was able to nab it? Primo would've caught that boar twice as fast as her if he'd gotten a second chance!

That dirty rotten Rosa, always stealing his glory. She shouldn't even have been in the contest in the first place! It was for boys, not *girls*. And why were they making such a big deal out of her winning, anyway? Didn't they know she already won every race? Every feat of strength? Big deal if she won this, too!

As usual, Isidora wanted to leave the party early, and for once Primo went with her. Everyone else is now asleep except Poppa, and who knows when he will make it home, if he makes it home at all.

Poppa! Primo is the maddest at him. What father bets against his own son?

Even his magic ring betrayed Primo. It may have once saved him from a Manalonga, but it sure didn't help today!

All of a sudden, the room floods with light,

as the clouds part away from the moon like a curtain. A beam of pale light hits the head of Diana, and now Primo can see her marble face.

And he notices something.

Diana's face—it's different. She isn't looking down. She's looking **up**.

That's weird! Primo thinks. How could *that* have happened? He touches the statue fragment and pushes at it. It's loose.

Loose?

He puts both hands on the head and rocks it back and forth. He then draws the stone out of its resting place—***CREEEAK!***—and almost drops it to the floor. It's heavy!

He stares at the hole where the head had been. With the moonlight shining, he can see that there's something inside. Is it just a rock?

He sticks his hand in. It's not a rock.

What he pulls out is a jar. A small clay jar. It is plugged up by a cork and has some kind of liquid inside. Primo pulls out the cork and is hit by a smell. *Skeevo!*

It's so foul he stoppers the jar right back up again. What could it possibly be?

Then he realizes.

It's a jar of magic oil. **Witch oil**.

Unguento!

His heart skips a beat.

He knows who the Janara lives with.

The Janara lives with **HIM**!

4

TO TRAP A WITCH

"WAKE UP!"

Primo brings his head bolt upright. "I'm awake! I'm awake!"

"What is *wrong* with you, toad!" Isidora says. "Why did you sleep on a barrel?"

"I was tired," Primo says, rubbing his eyes.

"Yeah, I guess getting chased around by a boar will wear you out."

She smiles meanly.

He hates Isidora! Maybe if she were nicer Primo would let her in on the big secret. But she is the *last* person he'd tell about the unguento. She'd blab to the adults and make all kinds of trouble.

No, this secret is only for his cousins.

And he can't wait to tell them!

Primo had thought about running back to the party and bringing the jar for them to see. But what if the Janara came to use it and found the jar missing? That'd ruin any chance Primo had of catching them in the act, so he stayed up all night waiting for them. (Or tried to.)

At breakfast, Maria Beppina asks Primo how he's doing.

"I'm great!" Primo says.

"Oh good! I thought you might be upset about losing," she says. "To Rosa."

Primo leans over to whisper to Maria Beppina. "I found out something that more than makes up for it!" he says. "Meet me at the stand with the Twins and I'll tell you!"

Poppa never made it home last night, so Primo has to go in search of him. He finds him asleep on the pageant stage, still in costume, his mouth wide open in a snore. It's all Primo can do to drag him to the stand.

Opening up, Poppa is grumpy about being back at work after having spent such a glorious week working on the stage.

Not that he stays long. Before all the tomatoes are even laid out, he mumbles that he has to go do something.

"Official business," he says. "I'll be right back."

But Primo knows he won't.

Maria Beppina arrives before the Twins, and Primo tells her to wait there.

"I have to go grab something!" he says. "If the Twins come, don't let them leave!"

"What if a customer comes?" she calls after him.

"Don't let them leave either!"

Back at home, Isidora is outside weaving. Primo sneaks past her and—after checking to make sure Momma isn't around—grabs hold of the head of Diana and, twist, **CREEEAK**, grab, he has the jar. He puts the head back in place and returns to the stand as fast as he can.

By the time he gets there, the Twins have arrived.

Perfect.

Rosa comes at him all gloating, and Primo relishes ruining her moment.

He tells them what he found, and what it means.

"The Janara lives . . . with ME!"

He waits for them to be blown away.

But they are not.

"So where is this Janara oil, then?" Rosa says.

"It's right here!" Primo says, holding up the jar.

"*Skeevo!*" Rosa says after Primo uncorks it. "It **stinks**!"

"I know whose it is, too!" Primo says. "Nonna Jovanna's!"

"How do you know?" Emilio says.

"I just do!" Primo says. "It's gotta be hers!"

"Even if it is," Maria Beppina says, "it might just be one of her remedies. For growing hair or removing warts or something."

"Well, why would she *hide* it, then?" Primo says, putting on a sour face.

"That jar might not have been hidden by *anyone* we know," Emilio says. "It could've been in there for hundreds of years. Thousands even."

"Then how did the head of Diana get turned the wrong way?" Primo says, explaining how he found it. "Someone had to have just moved it!"

"Are you sure about that, donkey brains?" Rosa says. "Maybe you just forgot which way it was facing."

"Look, why can't you all just accept it? This is witch oil and someone in my family is a Janara!" Primo says. "And I know how to prove it!"

Primo's plan is simple.

Whoever put that jar in the wall also put the head of Diana back wrong. When Primo points out this mistake, the shocked and flustered look on the guilty person's face will tell him that *that* is who the Janara is.

"What head?" Nonna Jovanna says. "Of who?"

"That head of Diana right *there*," Primo says, pointing.

"Oh, look at that!" his grandmother says. "Why, I never noticed that before! Is it new?"

Primo asks Momma next. "What is this stupid nonsense?" she says. "It's the same as it's ever been!"

Poppa is even more emphatic.

"I've lived in this house my **entire** life and I promise you that that head has **always** been facing up!"

He crosses his arms to show that that's the end of it.

Has she always been facing up? Primo wonders. He starts to doubt himself.

But his parents never notice anything, and whoever the Janara is must also be a great liar, otherwise how could they have kept the secret all this time? And that liar *has* to be Nonna Jovanna!

Her whole *I-never-noticed-that-before* must be an act. Primo decides to ask her directly. Probably she won't even mind Primo finding out. Maybe she'll be happy! Primo is her favorite grandchild, after all. (It sure isn't Isidora.) Maybe she'll even show him some real spells!

"Look, Nonna," Primo says the next time he can get her alone. "I know."

"What?" she says, practically shouting.

"I know," he repeats, with a wink.

"You know what?"

"That you're a . . ." Primo looks around. And whispers: "*Janara.*"

"A tomato?" Nonna Jovanna says. "Why yes, I'd love a tomato, thank you!"

She then stirs some salt into the coffee she's making.

Maybe it's *not* her.

But who then?

It can't be Momma, Primo thinks. It just wouldn't be right for *mothers* to be Janara.

(Besides, the last time Primo tried asking her if she was a Janara, Momma chased him around with a frying pan trying to brain him .)

No, it makes much more sense that the Janara is Poppa.

After all, Poppa *does* act suspicious. He's never at the stand, and he's always getting Primo to lie to Momma for him. And just where does he go all the time? He always claims it's related to business, but Primo knows that's never true either.

The only way to find out is to secretly follow him.

Maria Beppina wants no part of it, and not Emilio either. Rosa, however, is game.

The next morning they meet early. When Poppa goes off, Primo and Rosa sneak after him, leaving Maria Beppina in charge of the stand.

Poppa claimed to be going to Vipera to settle his account with the oil presser, but he doesn't even turn down the street that leads to the arch. Instead, he doubles back around and returns to the Triggio, ending up at Renzo the Barber's.

Poppa sits down for a shave and then he and

Renzo switch places, with the barber playing the mandolin in the chair while Poppa rubs Renzo's bald head and sings.

That done, Poppa heads out in the direction of the Twins', stopping at the Tavern at the Fork. He buys some lotto tickets and sits down for a few rounds of the Game of the Goose with the old men who always hang around there.

Next, Poppa heads out back to play bocce in the dusty courtyard. After three games, he walks farther on down the lane to the wine-maker's, where he has a couple of glasses of rosolio, lies down under a fig tree, and takes a nap.

"Okay," Rosa says to Primo as they walk back to the stand. "The Janara is definitely **not** your dad."

That night, Poppa brings home eel for dinner. When Momma starts to complain, Poppa tells her how much money he won from betting on Rosa. Momma actually throws her arms around Poppa and kisses him.

Skeevo.

"Let that be a lesson to you, son," Poppa says to Primo. "Never underestimate a girl."

"Yeah, little brother," Isidora says. "Especially one who always kicks your butt!"

Primo is grumpy beyond grumpy.

"If only you knew what I know," Primo says under his breath.

"What did you say, toad?"

"Nothing," Primo grumbles.

It's hot and miserable in the kitchen, which just adds to the misery Primo feels inside, so he gobbles down the eel and excuses himself to bed.

The worst part is that Primo is starting to think that Emilio and Maria Beppina are right. Maybe that jar *has* been in that wall for a thousand years. Or maybe it's not unguento at all. None of his family could possibly be a Janara. They're all just too . . . *themselves.* He bangs his head against the pillow, thinking that nothing amazing is ever going to happen to him.

But he's wrong.

Something amazing *is* about to happen to him. Right now.

Are you ready for it?

It may be the steamy July heat that keeps Primo from sleeping soundly, or maybe that sound would wake him up no matter what.

CREEEAK.

He sits up with a start. He **knows** that noise.

The head of Diana is being moved!

Is anyone missing from the bed? It's too dark to tell.

He himself gets out of the bed, quietly.

He creeps along the dirt floor, quietly.

In the kitchen, someone is carefully placing the head of Diana down on the ground.

They are reaching into the wall.

They are pulling out the jar.

The cork pops, and the smell of the unguento reaches Primo from across the room.

The person turns to the moonlight to see what they are doing.

And Primo sees their face.

5

THE JANARA IS . . .

"ISIDORA!"

She looks just as shocked as her brother.

"You! *You're* the Janara!" Primo says. "I can't believe it!"

"What? **No!**" Isidora says.

"Then why are you holding that jar of witch oil?" Primo says.

"This? This isn't witch oil! This is just medicine that Nonna Jovanna gave me," Isidora says. "For when I can't sleep!"

"I have to say, you're a lot cooler than I thought, being a Janara and all," Primo says. "And the way you kept it a secret! Wow! I can't wait to tell everyone!"

A look of terror comes to Isidora's face

"You can't!" she says. "You can't tell *anyone*!"

"A-**ha**!" Primo says. "So you admit it! You *are* a Janara!"

Primo grabs her by the hair.

"**OW!**" Isidora says, playing tug-of-war with her own braids. "What are you doing!?"

"I grabbed a Janara by the hair!" Primo says. "Now you have to do whatever I say!"

"No, I don't, you toad!" she says, and slugs

him in the stomach. He lets go. "That's just an old wives' tale!"

Isidora's whole attitude changes. She turns angry and points a finger in Primo's face.

"Now, you listen to me, little brother," she says threateningly. "You don't breathe a word of this to anyone, not even the cousins. If you do, I'll turn you into a *real* toad!" She steps in closer, so their faces almost touch. "And don't think I can't!"

Primo tries to fake a brave smile, but he can't quite muster it. After all, his sister has beaten him up plenty, so he knows she doesn't mind doing it. And if she starts doing it with magic—*Janara* magic!—he could really be in trouble.

"What are you two doing!"

Primo and Isidora turn to see Momma.

"Did you hear what we were talking about?" Primo asks.

"What you were *talking* about?" Momma says. "Why are you two talking at all! It's the middle of the night! Go back to bed and BE QUIET!"

"Yes," Isidora says, leaning into Primo. "Be quiet!"

She draws down her lower eyelid and follows Momma back to bed.

Primo, however, is too excited for sleep.

A Janara! His own sister is a real live **Janara**!

6

WHO'S THE DONKEY BRAINS NOW?

AT breakfast this morning, Primo is *dying* to ask Isidora some questions! Isidora, however, seems less than excited to talk to Primo. In fact, when their eyes meet, Isidora's are burning. With anger.

After Momma complains about their being up in the middle of the night, Maria Beppina asks why. Primo looks over into Isidora's furious eyes and mumbles some excuse.

At the stand, the Twins come to make their deliveries, and Rosa is talking about how maybe the Janara is Uncle Tommaso. Oh, how Primo wants to tell her the truth—tell both of them!—but he can't.

So he shrugs and mumbles again.

"Well, we'll see you later," Emilio says, climbing into the ox-cart. "Our uncle Zino is taking us to play bocce this afternoon if you want to come...."

Alone, Primo's head spins with thoughts. Nervous thoughts, thrilled thoughts. And questions for Isidora! So many questions.

Like:

WHEN did you become a Janara?

HOW did you become a Janara?

WHAT are your powers?

WHERE is the Tree of the Janara?

WHO goes there at night?

Oh, Primo is just bursting with questions!

And then he sees her—Isidora! Walking up to the stand.

There are a couple of customers milling about, old ladies who take forever to shop, squeezing everything three times before buying anything. Isidora says she's there to help and is all smiles with the ancient women. But the moment they're gone, she turns ornery.

"I need you to promise me you'll keep your mouth shut, little brother," she says. "Promise!"

"Yeah, yeah, sure," Primo says, and launches into his questions. *WHEN—HOW—WHAT—WHERE?* he asks, not even leaving time for her to answer.

Not that she is going to answer him. The only thing she's going to do is lose her temper.

"Primo, you *don't* underst—"

"Does it run in the family?" Primo says. "Will I become a Janara when I'm older, too?"

"No way, toad!" she says. "It doesn't work like that."

Then he asks if he lost in the Boar Hunt because the Janara were helping Rosa. "Janara do that, you know!"

"No they don't," Isidora says. "You don't know anything. You lost because you're a scamorza head and you're not fast enough or strong enough!"

Before Primo can ask another question, Isidora cuts him off.

"You just don't get it, do you?" she says. "No more questions about this—**ever!** And if you breathe a word—so much as one tiny little word—to anyone, you'll be six inches tall and catching dinner with your tongue. Got it?"

Primo gulps. "Got it."

At the end of the day, the Twins are hanging out with Maria Beppina on her steps.

"We're about to head off to the bocce court," Emilio says. "You coming?"

While they walk out of town together, Rosa won't let it drop about Uncle Tommaso being a Janara.

Primo so badly wants to tell what he knows, he's bursting! But then he thinks about what flies must taste like and keeps his mouth shut.

"Ah, just forget it!" Primo finally says. "There *is* no Janara. Emilio's right. That old jar must have been in that wall for a hundred thousand years. And it's probably not even witch oil in the first place!"

Rosa looks surprised for a minute. Then she says, "Yeah, that has to be it. It probably was just another one of your dumb ideas." She makes the crazy gesture, twirling her fingers alongside her head. "Your *stupid* ideas, I mean. I should've realized it would all come to nothing the moment you showed us that jar."

It is already hot enough outside to fry an egg, but Primo feels his face burn hotter.

"In fact," Rosa says, "I bet you made the whole thing up! You probably stole that skeevo old jar from Nonna Jovanna and said you found it in the wall just to distract from me having won the Boar Hunt." She raised both arms in the air. "From being the CHAMPION of the WORLD!"

"Ah, shut your beak!" Primo says, practically exploding. "You're just the champion of some stupid game for kids!"

"Well, you're the champion of nothing!" Rosa says. "And you'll never know who the Janara is, you donkey brains!"

"I **do** know who the Janara is!" Primo says. "I just can't tell!"

Maria Beppina's eyes go wide. "You *do*?"

"Ah, phooey!" Rosa says. "Can't you see he's lying? Primo! He's always got to be the center of attention! The one with the best plan. Well, his dumb plan to find the Janara tree didn't work,

and he couldn't beat a girl at the Boar Hunt, so now he's just downright lying about stuff!"

"Am not!" Primo says.

"Well, then who is it?" Rosa says. "Donkey. *Brains.*"

"It's my sister!" Primo says. "It's **Isidora**! Now who's the donkey brains?"

Primo is happy for a moment, taking in the look of shock on all of their faces.

Then he thinks:

What did I just do?

IT'S ISIDORA!

7

GOADED BUT NOT
YET TOADED

THE head of Diana is on the floor, and Primo has the bottle of witch oil in his hand. He's trying to bring himself to use a couple of drops of it. Maybe it will turn him into a Janara? On the other hand, maybe his hair will turn blue and all his toes will fall off.

When he hears someone awake he quickly puts the head back.

"What are *you* doing up so early?" Momma says, walking in.

Following her is Isidora, who eyes him suspiciously.

Primo feels guilty about what he did. But why should he feel guilty? What's the harm,

anyway? If *he* was a Janara, he'd tell everyone! Besides, it wasn't fair to make him keep a secret like that. And if Isidora was so worried about someone finding out, she shouldn't have put the darn head back the wrong way.

But she keeps looking at him like she already knows he spilled the beans. Things get worse at breakfast. Maria Beppina comes down late looking sick. She doesn't sit next to Isidora like she always does and she can't look her in the face. *That Maria Beppina!* Primo thinks. *She's going to blow it!*

Isidora knows something is wrong—he can

see it! Primo really doesn't want to be a toad.

At the stand, the only thing the Twins want to talk about is Isidora being a Janara.

"Are you *sure* about this?" Emilio says. "She admitted it to you?"

"*Shhh-sh!*" Primo says. "You want someone to hear?"

"Don't be such a chicken!" Rosa says. "Isidora wouldn't really hurt you."

"She's nice to *you* guys," Primo says. "You have no idea how mean she really is! Why, I bet it was her playing all those tricks on you back in Mischief Season."

"Ah, phooey!" Rosa says.

"If she really is a Janara," Emilio says, "who knows what she might do to us to keep her secret?"

"But she's *Isidora*!" Maria Beppina says. "Isidora wouldn't hurt any of us."

Then Primo sees her—his sister! Heading straight for them!

"Shh! Guys, *shhh*! She's coming!"

Isidora is carrying a small crate. She nods hello and starts laying out figs.

The others don't speak, which feels suspicious, because why wouldn't they be speaking?
Primo searches his brain for something to say,
but he can't think of anything. What could
there possibly be to say?

Now Isidora must notice the awkward silence, because she's looking from one to the
other of them as she lays out the figs. Then she
stops.

"I don't believe it!" she says angrily. Isidora
gives a hard shove to the crate, sending figs
flying all over the street, and storms off.

The others look at each other.

"Well, um, we should really be getting back to the farm," Emilio says.

"Yeah," Rosa says, following him onto the cart. "Getting back."

Maria Beppina, all red-faced, hurries away too, leaving Primo alone.

And vulnerable.

He picks up the figs and dusts each one off, placing them on the counter carefully.

When the noon bell rings, he shuts down the stand as slowly as he possibly can. He does *not* want to go home for lunch. But he has to.

And when he does, Isidora is waiting outside the door for him.

"Oh, hey," Primo says. "I picked those figs up off the ground for you."

Isidora punches him in the stomach. Hard.

"You think this is a **game**?" Isidora says. "You told Maria Beppina! You told the *Twins*!"

"Did not!" Primo says, doubled over.

"Then why were they looking at me like I

had three heads and I wanted to eat them?"

"Well, your face does have that—hey! *OW!!*"

Isidora is pinching and twisting his skin so hard he has to get down onto his knees.

"Look, they guessed! I couldn't help it. I would *never* have told them!" Primo says, begging from the ground. "You aren't going to turn me into a toad, are you?"

Isidora lets go.

Primo's arm is red where she was twisting it. "That really hurt!"

"Good!" Isidora says. "Consider it just the beginning."

"Why do you even care that those guys know?" Primo says, getting up. "It's so cool that you're a Janara! If it was me, I'd tell everyone!"

"No, you **wouldn't**," Isidora says. "Not if you wanted to stay alive."

"What are you *talking* about?"

Isidora shakes her head. Suddenly, she doesn't even seem mad.

WAIT!

"You don't understand anything, Primo," she says, and walks over to him.

Isidora reaches a hand toward his throat and Primo hops back, scared. But she isn't moving to choke him. She's just taking hold of what is hanging around his neck.

"This ring," she says. "You think it's magic. You think it saved you from the Manalonga. It didn't do anything. *I* saved you from the Manalonga. And I had to pay for it, too."

Then Isidora turns and walks away.

"Wait! What do you mean, *you* had to pay for it?" Primo says, calling after her.

But she's gone.

WHAT DO YOU MEAN, *YOU* HAD TO PAY FOR IT?

8

CONVERSATION WITH
A MONSTER

THE thing with Isidora is that she used to not be so mean.

Once, she was a great big sister. In fact, Primo idolized her. They used to do everything together. But then one day she started being angry and annoyed all the time and wouldn't let him hang around her anymore.

Everyone said that was just what happens with big sisters, but now Primo isn't so sure. What if she started acting all different because she had become a Janara? Maybe becoming a Janara turns a person mean?

Not that Isadora is *totally* mean. She still helps Primo with some things. Like the costume.

And the Manalonga.

Except Primo isn't sure he believes it. Because it was his ring that saved him that day, wasn't it? His magic ring!

At breakfast, he wants to ask Isidora about it, but he can't get her alone. Then she and Maria Beppina head off to the mill to make a delivery.

Primo leaves, too. He goes in the other direction, however. Toward the bridge.

The bridge where he dared the Manalonga.

Zi Paulo, the farmer who lives next to the Twins, is coming the other way when he gets there. His cartload of hay takes up nearly the entire bridge, and Primo waits for him to pass.

The skinny farmer nods to Primo as he passes, and now Primo walks slowly up the ramp of the bridge, carefully sticking to the middle. The safety zone.

Near the top, he hears a voice from over the side.

Hey, Primo! Primo, is that you? It's the voice

of Dino. *Hey, Primo! You've gotta come check this out! I found a snake in the mud under the bridge. It's huge! It's gotta be six feet long. I think it's dead but I'm not sure. Can you come look?*

"I know it's not Dino!" Primo yells from the center of the bridge. "I know it's you, Manalonga!"

Manalonga! Hah! the voice says. *No, it's really me! Dino! Come look! I think it's starting to move.*

The freaky thing is how much it *does* sound like Dino.

"Look, Manalonga, you're not gonna trick me!" Primo shouts. "I just want to ask you a question!"

What? the voice says. Still like Dino.

"That day I leaned over the edge and dared you to grab me," Primo says. "Why didn't you do it?"

I have no idea what you're talking about!

They keep going back and forth like this, with Primo asking questions and the Manalonga insisting it's Dino.

Finally, Primo tries a different approach.

I JUST WANT TO ASK YOU A QUESTION!

"All I want to know
is what *scared* you so much that day!"
he says. "Was it my ring? Or something else?"

Suddenly, the voice under the bridge turns
ugly and horrible—like bats screeching. It no
longer even sounds human.

*You think I am afraid of **anything**?* the now
vicious voice says. *I know why you're here, you
sniveling brat. And I know why you came that
day, too!*

The hideous voice laughs, an awful sound
that sets the hairs on the back of Primo's neck
standing on end.

*Your ring! You're so stupid you think it's magic—you think it's **my** ring! Well, there is no magic in that ring of yours. It was your sister who saved your life that day.* The Manalonga lets out a sound of disgust. *I was **so close** to grabbing you—I could feel it! And then that horrid Janara made it hail and pulled you away! She wasn't supposed to do that, you know. She broke a rule. A very basic rule!*

"What rule?"

Janara aren't allowed to use their magic during the day, you stupid fool! And not in their human form, either. It cost her dearly to save your life, and how do you repay her? By telling her secret! Oh, what the other Janara will do to her if ever they find out! Hah-hah-hah!

"What do you mean?" Primo says.

Didn't you **believe** *your sister when she told you that you had to shut up about her!?*

Primo is so confused. He's not quite sure what it all means—or if he even *wants* to understand what it all means.

"Why should I believe *you*?" Primo says. "You just hide down there all day hoping to snatch a kid! How would you know anything about what goes on up here? Or with the Janara?"

The Manalonga laughs again. *There's nothing I don't know. How do you think I can imitate every single person you ever met?*

The voice changes.

What you were talking *about? Why are you two talking at all!*

It's Momma's voice. Primo gets another chill.

"Even if you *do* know everything," Primo says, "how do I know you're telling the truth about what Isidora did for me?"

That's the fantastic thing, the voice says, now back to its horrible tone. *You don't! Ha! HA-HAHAHAHAHAHA!!!!*

The laughing follows Primo back down the ramp until it becomes just the sound of rushing water. But even then, he can still hear it.

The laughing.

Primo wants to tell Isidora everything. About how sorry he is—about how he'll make it all better. But she and Maria Beppina get back so late from the mill, Primo never gets a chance to talk to her alone. The next day, they're supposed to go do laundry together, but Momma tells Isidora to stay home and help scrub the pots.

At the river, all the cousins are there, including Sergio, who hasn't been around since the boar gored him. His ribs are bandaged up, but otherwise he seems fine.

"Hey, where's you-know-*who*?" Rosa says to Primo.

"We-know-*what*?" Sergio says.

"Oh, right, you weren't here!" Rosa says, excited to get to tell someone the big secret.

"It's Isidora. She's a—"

"**Hey!**" Primo says, stopping her. "You can't tell him!"

"What? But it's Sergio!" Rosa says. "He's gonna find out sooner or later."

"Find out what?" Sergio says.

"*ThatIsidoraisaJanara!*" Rosa hurries to say, and then sticks out her tongue at Primo.

The only good thing is that Sergio doesn't believe it.

"Isidora is just messing with you," Sergio says. "What a bunch of idiots!"

Maria Beppina leaves, but the others argue back and forth over whether or not Isidora really is a Janara.

Primo does the laundry as fast as he can—for once!—and hurries to get home. He finds Isidora, but now she's with Maria Beppina. Why can't he ever get her alone!

Finally, he does. He goes to tell her that he finally understands, but Isidora cuts him off.

"Look, Primo," she says, her whole manner changed. "It really isn't fair that I haven't answered any of your questions."

"It isn't?" Primo says, surprised.

"No, it's not," she says. "You are my

little brother, and it was my mistake that you found what you found. So I want to share with you what it's like."

"What *what* is like?" Primo says.

"Being a Janara."

Primo can't believe it.

"You *have* always wanted to go the tree, haven't you?" Isidora says. "The Tree of the Janara?"

"Well, sure," Primo says. "But after what you said . . ."

"If you really want to go, I'll take you," Isidora says. "You and our cousins, too. Tell them to meet me on the watchtower wall in three days. At the eleventh hour."

"What about everything you said? About not telling anyone your secret?"

"They already know my secret. What's important is that they don't tell it to anyone *else*. And after you go to the tree . . ." Isidora pauses. "Well, let's just say I don't think any of you will be telling secrets."

9

A CHAPTER YOU REALLY SHOULDN'T READ IF YOU DON'T LIKE BEING TERRIFIED

THE three days take forever to pass. Primo keeps asking Isidora what it is going to be like at the tree, but she won't tell him a thing. All she ever replies is: "You'll see."

The cousins arrive at the watchtower together to await the eleventh hour bell. Maria Beppina looks like she'd rather be anywhere but here, she's so afraid of what's about to happen.

Sergio, on the other hand, is treating the whole thing like it's a big joke.

BONG-be-BONG-BONG!

The bells peal, and at the same instant, Isidora appears. Her timing is so perfect it's spooky!

"Are all of you ready?" she says, the eleventh hour still tolling. "To go to the Tree of the Janara?"

BONG-be-BONG-BONG!

"I, uhm, er," Maria Beppina says. "I just, well…"

She can't stop hemming and hawing.

Isidora shakes her head. "Go *home*, Maria Beppina," she says, taking pity on her.

Maria Beppina breathes a sigh of relief and hurries down the tower steps.

"Well?" Isidora says. "Are any of the rest of you brave enough?"

"Sure we are!" Sergio says, charging ahead. "Let's go!"

Primo and Rosa follow behind Sergio and

Isidora. Emilio pauses like he's thinking about joining Maria Beppina, but he's too curious not to come, and he brings up the rear.

Isidora leads them to the bridge, but rather than turn left to go downriver, she heads in the opposite direction, through a thicket of reeds.

"Isn't the tree the other way?" Emilio says. "At the Bridge of Ancient Ages?"

"That's just another old wives' tale," Isidora says, pushing her way through the tall water grasses.

The night is already stormy, but now the wind turns violent, whipping the reeds into their faces. It feels like a summer thunderstorm is just about to hit.

"Maybe we should turn back," Emilio says.

"I knew you'd be scared," Isidora says.

"We're not scared!" Sergio says.

"Dang right we're not!" Rosa says. Her eyes don't agree with what her mouth is saying, however.

As they keep walking, Emilio says, "Hey, aren't we going around in a circle?"

"No," Isidora says. "It only seems like it."

Primo is completely lost by the time they get out of the thick brush. They climb up a wooded hill until they reach the edge of a meadow. The grass stretches out to a sky showing the last hints of sunlight. On the horizon stands an enormous walnut tree. Beneath it, a fire burns.

Primo feels himself gulp.

"There it is," Isidora says, pointing. "The tree! To get there I suggest you do not go through the open field. Witches don't like to be snuck up on. Follow the path through the woods and it will lead you to the far side of the tree. "

She turns and starts walking back the other way.

"Wait!" Primo says. "Where are you going?"

"Home. I have to go change into a Janara, remember?" Isidora turns back and smiles, a gleam in her eyes. "Don't worry. I'll see you **there**!"

A moment later, she's gone.

The four cousins huddle.

"I'm cold," Emilio says. "Is anyone else cold?"

"Is this really a good idea?" Rosa says. "Or are we all being a bunch of donkey brains?"

"Hah! I never thought I'd see it—the famous Rosa, scared!" Sergio says, stalking off ahead. "Well, I've been waiting my whole life to see

the Janara, and I'm not heading back now because of a bunch of scared little kids!"

"Hey! Who are you calling *little*?" Rosa says.

They all shake their heads at the new Sergio.

The path through the trees is twisty and
dark, and they keep having to re-find the way.
Finally, they come to the edge of the woods, like
Isidora said they would.

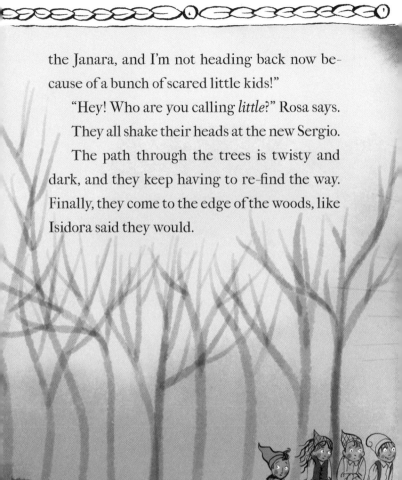

The towering walnut tree stands at
the peak of the meadow, a dark shadow
against the starry sky. Beneath it, the fire
blazes away, throwing light on a group of

animals circling the tree. They look like sheep or goats, except that people are *riding* them.

People—or **witches**?

"It's now or never," Rosa says.

Primo nods. But he doesn't move.

"Well, I'm going!" Sergio says.

As soon as he takes a step, however, there is a loud crashing. And again!

The crashing noise gets louder. And then there's a spooky sound, like from some kind of strange trumpet.

"Maybe this wasn't such a good idea . . ." Sergio says, carefully backing up along the path they came in on.

The others start to back up, too.

A stick breaks.

"Where are you *gooooing*?" a voice from behind them says.

The four cousins jump out of their skins and turn to see a hooded figure. They quickly turn to run back the other way, but they are blocked by someone—or *something*—else.

Another creature! This one is also hooded, and holding a big blazing torch.

What *are* these monsters? Janara? Or some other, more *sinister* kind of witch?

The second one moves a step closer, and the fire lights up its face. Its face! It looks like some

kind of horned demon gorilla! It's *gruesome!*
Hideous! And the skin on its face, it's so red—
red like **blood**.

And then the face—it goes away.

"AHHH! Its face—its face just fell off!!!"
Sergio screams.

And then he faints, dropping to the ground
with a **thud**!

"Sergio!" Primo says, rushing to him.

As Primo pulls him up off the ground, Sergio's eyes open back up.

"What's going on?" he says, all groggy. "Where am I?"

"You are somewhere you do not belong!" the first hooded figure says. "Tell me, children, **WHY** should we let you live? Live, so you can tell the secrets of the Janara!"

"We won't tell anyone!" Rosa says, blubbering in terror along with the others. "We p-p-p-promise!"

"You must do more than promise. You must **swear**!" the creature says. "*Double* swear!"

They all put their hands over their hearts and spit and say, "I swear!"

"You will never breathe a word of what you have learned to anyone. You will not even talk about this with each other! And if you do—if you reveal *anything* you know of any Janara— there is only one punishment!"

"D-d-d-d-death?" Sergio says, on the verge of tears. Suddenly he's the old Sergio again .

"**No!** A fate worse than death!"

"But what's worse than . . ." Emilio says, and gulps. "Death?"

"You don't want to know!" the horrible hooded figure says. "**Swear again!**"

They all swear again.

"Just remember—we can come get you!" the figure says. "*Wherever* you are!"

The figure looks at the four children, holding each other, cowering, and says:

"Now **run**!"

They all race back home.

Screaming!

Life goes on, but our book is done!

So now you have it! You have seen a real liveJanara! *Two* Janara, in fact!

OR have you?

Things are never how they appear in Benevento, even when you think you are IN on the secret.

But wait! What's this? There's another chapter! Oops! Excuse us for rushing the ending.

Now let's have a look at what's left, shall we?

Sigismondo

RAFAELLA

BRᵁᴺᴼ

S.   R.   B.

10
CODA

"YOU'RE being awfully quiet this morning," Poppa says to Primo.

He nods silently.

Primo is pretty sure he will never speak again. Speaking can only get him into trouble with . . . *them.*

Isidora, however, is positively chatty at breakfast. And hungry. She reaches across the table for another slice of bread, but Momma grabs her hand before she can get it.

"Isidora, what happened to you?" Momma says. "Are you *bleeding?*"

"No!" Isidora says. "What are you talking about?"

Momma turns Isidora's hand over. Across her palm is a bright red streak.

"Well, it's something," Momma says.

"It's just some dye—from the other day when I went to the mill."

"I didn't see it on you yesterday."

"What else would it be?" Poppa says in his annoyed-at-Momma-for-worrying voice.

Isidora gets up and washes the red off. It's a color that Primo recognizes. In fact, he will never forget it.

It was the color of the face of the Janara.

Of a mask.

All day, Primo doesn't say anything to Isidora about knowing. He might have been mad at her, but he understands. In fact, he thinks it's funny.

Isidora tricked them! It was all

staged—she terrified him and the others into keeping quiet so they'll never tell her secret.

It's fan-*tas*-tic! Now Primo doesn't have to worry or feel guilty anymore.

That night, the heat is so bad that the whole family goes to sleep in their underwear. The wind whooshes and howls, so much so it rattles the shutters and wakes Primo up. He looks over next to him.

Isidora isn't there.

Primo decides to get up and watch her put on the Janara oil . But this time he won't interrupt.

He doesn't get the chance, however, because Isidora is already coming back to bed.

Did she not use the oil?

"Hey! Hey, sis!" Primo whispers.

She doesn't respond. Instead, she gets back into bed and lies down, her eyes shut.

"Hey!" Primo says, shaking her. "Isidora, come on! Quit playing! I know you're awake. You were just walking!"

But there is no getting her up.

Primo even tries lifting up her eyelids, but it's like he can barely see her eyes, they're so far back in her head. For a moment he panics—is she dead?—but then he realizes she's breathing.

She is in some sort of trance, like Sleeping Beauty. Is this what happens when a person becomes a Janara? But what about their bodies turning into wind?

Primo stays awake, nervous. The shutters rattling and slamming make him jumpy. Finally, the storm quiets. He hears a gasp.

It's Isidora.

Her eyes are open.

He smiles at her.

She smiles back.

"Does it hurt?" Primo leans in to whisper so as not to wake the others. "Becoming a . . ." He still doesn't want to say the word.

She shakes her head. "No, not really," she says. "Not at all, actually."

"Did you do any mischiefs tonight?"

"No, I'm not really that kind of—" She stops

herself and smiles. "You know."

They just lie there a moment, in silence. Then Primo asks:

"Do you think there really is no chance that I'll become one, too?"

"To be honest, Primo, I have no idea." Isidora takes hold of his hand. "I think you have the same chance as I did. The same as anybody. Maybe better."

Should Primo tell her that he knows about her trick? And say that it doesn't matter? That he really won't tell anyone.

But saying that will only make him feel better. Isidora will feel better if she thinks her trick worked.

So Primo gives his sister a kiss, turns over, and goes to sleep.

Life goes on, but NOW our book is done!

Life was very different in Benevento in the 1820s.

HERE'S HOW THEY LIVED: TIME

- ✥ Most people never looked at a clock.

- ✥ If you lived near a church, you would know what time it was by the pattern of the bells ringing.

- ✥ If you lived in the countryside, you would tell time by looking at the sun. Its path across the sky was divided into twelve hours in the same way a ruler is divided into twelve inches.

✧ Instead of noon coming at 12:00, it came at the sixth hour, because it was when the sun was halfway across the sky. The first hour was the one after sunrise, and the eleventh the one before sunset.

✧ The hour grew or shrank depending on the time of year, because it was $\frac{1}{12}$th of however long the sun was out. So in Benevento, an hour in late June would last 75 of our minutes, while at Christmas it would last for only 46 of them.

If you want to learn MORE, please visit witchesofbenevento.com.

HISTORICAL NOTE

Witches have a history, too. And since the 1820's, the ones of Benevento have been in steep decline.

While the city is still associated with magical beings and events, now even the citizens of Benevento imagine their witches to be the black-hatted, broomstick-riding sort that have been imported from the English-speaking world, and not their own home-grown variety.

What is special about the mythological universe of Benevento is how unique it is. Benevento has forever been a crossroads, a place where tree-worshipping Germans mingled with the followers of Greek Hecate, Roman Diana, and Egyptian Isis, and myths like those of the Sirens were carried in and out of town. All of of these ancient influences took root vibrantly here, producing the inimitable folklore of the janara, the Manalonga, and the Clopper.

ACKNOWLEDGMENTS

The one source that stands above all others—and the person who has done the most to keep the mythology of Benevento alive—is Paola Caruso. Paola has documented the mythology of the region, including the experiences of her own mother, who grew up in the Triggio. Without her, this series would not exist.

As far as what the janara might have actually been like, our main source is Carlo Ginzburg's *I benandanti*, which uses records from long-ago witch trials to examine the ancient—and secret—religious rituals of rural Italy. The scene of Primo's family chasing an eel, on the other hand, was inspired by Carmine d'Agostino's memoir of life in the poorest part of Benevento, *Il mio Triggio*. For understanding what the state of learning in Catholic lands were, we consulted George Borrow's 1830s travelogue, *The Bible in Spain*. And beyond literary sources, the contemporary prints and drawings of artists like Gaetano Dura and Achille Vianelli were vital to our understanding early 19th c. life in the region.

To them—and those we are unable to mention—we offer our most sincere thanks.

Read all the books in the

WITCHES of

series!

MISCHIEF SEASON:
A Twins Story

Emilio and Rosa are tired of all the nasty tricks the Janara are playing when they ride at night making mischiefs. Maybe the fortune-teller Zia Pia will know how to stop the witches.

THE ALL-POWERFUL RING:
A Primo Story

Primo wants to prove he is the bravest, but will the ring really protect him from all danger—even from the Manalonga, who hide in wells and under bridges?

BEWARE THE CLOPPER!:
A Maria Beppina Story

Maria Beppina, the timid tagalong cousin, is also the slowest runner of the five. She is always afraid that the Clopper, the old witch who chases the children, will catch her. She's also curious, so one day she decides to stop—just stop—and see what the Clopper will do.

BENEVENTO

RESPECT YOUR GHOSTS:
A Sergio Story

Sergio is in charge of Bis-Bis, the ancestor spirit who lives upstairs. Unfortunately, it's hard to satisfy all of the ghost's demands and still keep Sergio's mother happy.

RUNAWAY ROSA:
A Twins Story

The Benevento children are excitedly preparing for the annual Boar Hunt, where the prize is given to the ten-year-old who catches the boar. No girl has ever competed, but Rosa is determined to take part—and win!

THE SECRET JANARA:
A Primo Story

Primo has been given a tantalizing clue about the secret Janara: the Janara lives with him! How can he discover who it is? Late one night he is successful.

JOHN BEMELMANS MARCIANO

I grew up on a farm taking care of animals. We had one spectacularly nice chicken, the Missus, who lived in a stall with an ancient horse named Gilligan, and one rooster, Leon, who pecked our heads on our way home from school. Leon, I have no doubt, was a demon. Presently I take care of two cats, one dog, and a daughter.

SOPHIE BLACKALL

I've illustrated many books for children, including the Ivy and Bean series. I drew the pictures in this book using ink made from black olives and goat spit. In 2016, I received a shiny gold Caldecott Medal for *Finding Winnie*. I grew up in Australia, but now my boyfriend and I live in Brooklyn with a cat who never moves and a bunch of children who come and go like the wind.